For my family and everyone at Victoria House

First published in the United States 1997
by Dial Books for Young Readers
A Division of Penguin Books USA Inc.
375 Hudson Street
New York, New York 10014

Published in the United Kingdom 1997
by David Bennett Books Limited
as *Cosy Moments with Teddy Bear*

Printed in Hong Kong
First Edition
1 3 5 7 9 10 8 6 4 2

Library of Congress Cataloging in Publication Data available upon request.
ISBN 0-8037-2076-9

The art for this book was rendered in oil.

Good Times
—with—
Teddy Bear

Jacqueline McQuade

Dial Books for Young Readers · New York

Eating breakfast in bed

Teddy Bear started his Saturday with a special treat—breakfast in bed. He tried very hard not to get his paws sticky or drop any crumbs on the sheets.

Playing outside

Teddy put on his favorite wool sweater and went out into the crisp fall air. He and his cat played hide-and-seek and kicked through the fallen leaves.

Sipping hot soup

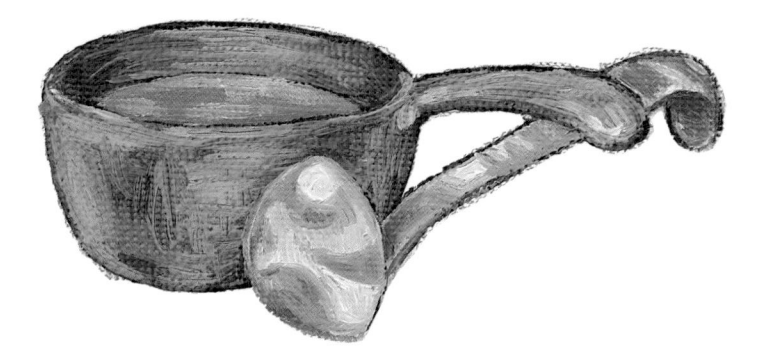

Teddy was chilly when he got back inside. The warmth of the kitchen and a mug of hot soup helped warm him.

Painting
a picture

Teddy sat by the living-room fire and painted a picture of
a house. His cat watched closely as Teddy swirled paint
into puffy white clouds.

Baking cookies

Teddy's mom carefully took the baking sheet out of the oven and put it on the table to cool. The sweet smell of chocolate-chip cookies filled the air. Teddy could hardly wait to taste one!

Having a tea party

Teddy hosted a tea party for his cat. He told magical stories and snacked on yummy treats.

Playing checkers

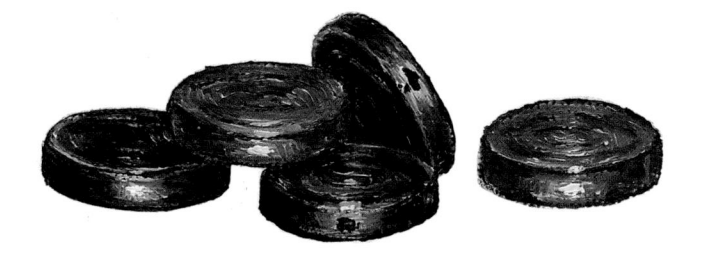

Teddy liked to play checkers with his dad.
He was quickly learning all the best moves.

Watching the sunset

Teddy sat quietly with his cat in the glow of the setting sun.
How big and beautiful the sun is! he thought.

Snuggling in a soft towel

After a hot bath, Teddy wrapped himself in a warm,
fluffy towel. His cat purred beside him.

Reading
a book

Teddy was getting tired, so he read a bedtime story to his cat.
"This will make you feel as sleepy as I am," he said.

Cuddling with Mom

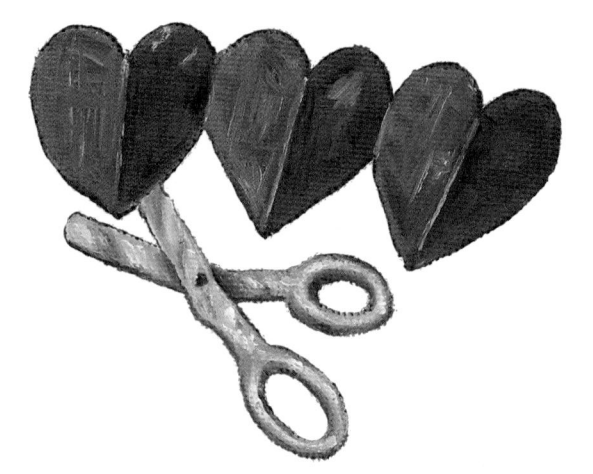

Teddy climbed up into his mom's lap. She gave him a big hug and whispered, "I love you, Teddy."

Tucked
in bed

Teddy and his cat happily nestled into bed. What a full
day they'd shared! Teddy drifted off to sleep, dreaming
of what tomorrow might bring.